SPACE RACE

MALORIE BLACKMAN

Illustrated by Colin Mier

www.randomhousechildrens.co.uk

For Neil and Lizzie, with love

SPACE RACE
A CORGI BOOK 978 0 552 56893 7

Published in Great Britain by Corgi Books,
an imprint of Random House Children's Publishers UK
A Random House Group Company

Corgi Pups edition published 1997
This Colour First Reader edition published 2013

1 3 5 7 9 10 8 6 4 2

The Random House Group Limited supports the Forest Stewardship Council (FSC®),
the leading international forest certification organization. Our books carrying the FSC
label are printed on FSC®-certified paper. FSC is the only forest certification scheme
endorsed by the leading environmental organizations, including Greenpeace. Our paper
procurement policy can be found at www.randomhouse.co.uk/environment.

Set in Bembo MT Schoolbook 21/28pt

Corgi Books are published by Random House Children's Publishers UK,
61–63 Uxbridge Road, London W5 5SA

www.**randomhousechildrens**.co.uk
www.**randomhouse**.co.uk

Addresses for companies within The Random House Group Limited can be found at:
www.randomhouse.co.uk/offices.htm

THE RANDOM HOUSE GROUP Limited Reg. No. 954009

A CIP catalogue record for this book is available from the British Library.

Printed in Italy.

Contents

COLOUR FIRST READER books are perfect for beginner readers. All the text inside this Colour First Reader book has been checked and approved by a reading specialist, so it is the ideal size, length and level for children learning to read.

Series Reading Consultant: Prue Goodwin
Honorary Fellow of the University of Reading

OUR SOLAR SYSTEM

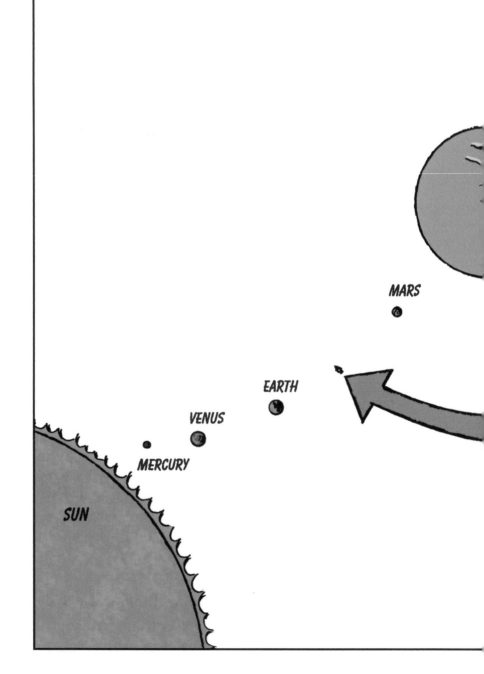

MARS

EARTH

VENUS

MERCURY

SUN

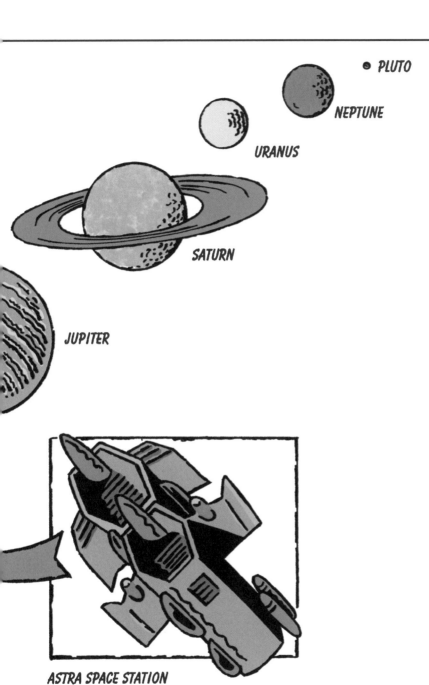

PLUTO

NEPTUNE

URANUS

SATURN

JUPITER

ASTRA SPACE STATION

Chapter One
The Challenge

Lizzie loved living on the Astra Space Station. All her friends on Earth were so jealous when her family moved out there. Lizzie had soon made lots of new friends and it was great fun. There was just one problem. Jake! All he did was brag and show off.

Today he was at it again, boasting about his brand new, super duper, fat-ace, deluxe spaceship. "It's got the latest computer so all I have to do is tell it where I want to go and when I want to get there and the computer does the rest. And my new ship's fast because it runs on diamond fuel.

It's one of the first ships
anywhere on this space station to
run on diamond fuel," said Jake.

Huh! If he was any more
pleased with himself he'd pop
like a balloon, Lizzie thought to
herself.

"I bet I've got the best spaceship in the whole school," Jake continued. He looked around the classroom. "It's a lot better than any of your ships, that's for sure."

Lizzie had had enough. "Jake, I bet my ship could beat yours any day."

The words were out of Lizzie's mouth before she could stop them. Jake burst out laughing – and he wasn't the only one. Some others in the class also creased up. Everyone else just looked at Lizzie as if she was seriously nuts!

"You must be joking!" Jake scoffed. "Your ship couldn't beat mine if I gave you one year's head start!"

"You don't have to give me a head start. My ship can beat yours any day of the week," said Lizzie, stubbornly.

"OK then. Let's have a race. Out to Pluto and back. The first one back to this classroom wins," said Jake.

Lizzie swallowed hard. Oops!

"Now you've done it!" whispered Lizzie's best friend, Sarah.

And Sarah was right! It was
one thing for Lizzie to say her
ship could beat Jake's, but it was
quite another to prove it. Lizzie's
spaceship was old and it only ran
on emerald fuel. Jake's ship ran
on diamond fuel so it travelled a
lot faster than hers ever could.

"I . . . I . . ."

"You're going to back out,
aren't you?" Jake
said smugly.

"No, I'm not going to back out. OK, you're on," said Lizzie. "We'll have our race this weekend."

"Oh no we won't. Let's have our race now," said Jake.

"But it's lunch-time," Lizzie protested. "We can't race to Pluto and still be back here for our first lesson after lunch."

"I can!" Jake smiled. "I can race to Pluto and back in about fifteen minutes!"

Lizzie's heart sank. She knew it would take her at least an hour and a half to get to Pluto and back. How could she get out of this?

"Jake, I hope Lizzie does beat you," said Naren. "Then maybe you won't show off so much."

"Yeah!"

"That's right!"

Lizzie smiled gratefully at her friends. At least they wanted her to win.

"She doesn't stand a chance and you all know it," Jake said with his usual smirk on his face.

"Jake, I'll race you, but let's have our race tomorrow – early. How about at seven o'clock in the morning?" said Lizzie. "I need to tune up my ship's engine first."

"That's fine by me," Jake shrugged. "And you can tune up your ship all you like – you'll still never beat me."

"We'll see about that," said Lizzie.

And she was determined that there was no way Jake was going

to win the race. He needed to
be taught a lesson. The only
trouble was – he was right. Lizzie
couldn't beat him. Not unless she
came up with a plan first.

Chapter Two
The Plan

Later that day after school, Lizzie and her friends gathered in the pizzeria. The space station had lots of different places to eat but they all liked pizzas the best. Lizzie gazed out of the window at the Earth below and sighed. What had she let herself in for now?

"So what're you going to do?"
Naren asked.

"I haven't a clue!" Lizzie sighed again and leaned her head on her cupped hand. She stared down at her dinner plate. She hadn't touched her Andorian beetle pizza and it was usually her favourite. She just didn't seem to have much of an appetite.

"Don't you want your dinner?"
Darla asked.

Lizzie shook her head.
Immediately, many different hands
reached into her plate for her
beetle pizza. Naren won!

He chewed on the pizza with
obvious relish, enjoying it
all the more for the look of
disappointment on his friends' faces.

"If you haven't got a plan,
why on earth did you want to
race at seven o'clock tomorrow
morning?" asked Darla.

"I was hoping Jake would say it
was too early!" Lizzie replied.

"No chance! Jake would
race you at three o'clock in the
morning if it gave him a chance
to show off!" sniffed Naren.

Just then, Sarah came into the pizzeria. She took a quick look around before making for Lizzie's table.

"D'you know what I just heard?" Sarah asked furiously.

Everyone shook their heads.

"No? What?"

"I left my pocket-PC in the classroom and I had to go back to get it so I could do my homework. But Jake and his friends were already there.

Lizzie, Jake's going to make sure that you don't win. He's going to sabotage your ship's engine tonight so there's no chance of your beating him."

"What a trog!" Darla exploded.

"You said it." Lizzie nodded vigorously. "He doesn't have to fix my ship. His ship could beat mine fair and square."

"Jake doesn't know the meaning of the word 'fair'," Sarah sniffed.

"We've got to teach him a lesson. We've *got* to! Come on, Lizzie – *think*!" Lizzie told herself sternly.

She had to come up with a plan, but what? And then it hit her – like an asteroid shower!

"I've got it! I've got it! I know how I can win this race and teach Jake a lesson once and for all," Lizzie told her friends.

They looked at each other.

"We're all ears!" said Sarah.

"Good! Because I can't do this without your help," said Lizzie.

"I'm going to need each and every one of you."

"We're with you, Lizzie," said Naren.

And they all gathered closer to hear Lizzie's plan.

Chapter Three
The Race Begins

The following morning, at seven o'clock precisely, Lizzie and Jake entered docking-bay three. Both of their ships were there, waiting for take-off.

"I'm surprised you bothered to
turn up," Jake told Lizzie.

"I'm going to win this race,"
smiled Lizzie.

"You've got space fever!" Jake
replied.

"We'll see!" Lizzie climbed into

her spaceship without another
word. Once they were both cleared
for take-off, the countdown began.

Five . . . four . . . three . . . two
. . . one! And they were off!

Jake roared ahead at once.
He veered towards Lizzie's ship,
forcing her to drop back or risk
being smashed into. Jake watched,
his hands relaxed behind his head
as Lizzie's ship fell further and
further behind.

By the time he had passed Mars, Lizzie's ship was no more than a small blip on his rear viewscreen. Jake slowed down his own ship. He certainly didn't have to hurry. Lizzie would never catch him now. He'd seen to that.

Jake spoke to his computer. "Computer, connect me through to Lizzie's ship."

Immediately Lizzie's face
appeared on the space
communicator.

"If you want to give up now,
you'd save us both a lot of time
and energy and you'd save
yourself a lot of humiliation,"
Jake told her.

Lizzie frowned at him. "Jake,
why on earth would I give up
when I'm ahead of you?"

"What're you talking about?" said Jake.

"Look out of your front viewscreen," said Lizzie. "I'm approaching Jupiter now. You should be able to see me ahead of you."

"You can't be ahead." Jake was stunned. "You were thousands of kilometres *behind* me."

"Not any more. I spent all of yesterday evening fine-tuning my ship and what's more I've got a secret weapon. You'll never catch me," grinned Lizzie.

Jake looked. And sure enough, up ahead in the distance was Lizzie's ship.

"What's your secret weapon? How did you pass me?" Jake was furious.

"Temper! Temper!" Lizzie teased. "If you'll admit defeat now and say my ship is better

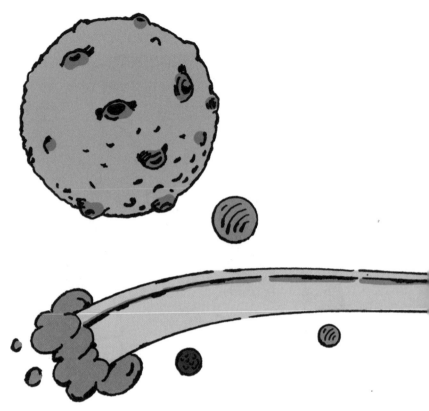

than yours then we don't have
to go any further."

"No way!" said Jake.
"Computer, set course for Pluto
at the maximum speed."

Jake's ship lurched forward
and started to race towards
Jupiter. In less than five minutes,

Jake passed Lizzie's ship. He still couldn't understand how Lizzie had passed him but it wouldn't happen again.

The next stop was Saturn and after that, Lizzie wouldn't see him for space dust!

Chapter Four
Beaten!

Jake waited until he passed Saturn before slowing down again. Beaming like a light beacon, he reconnected with Lizzie's ship.

"I don't know how you got ahead of me just now but it doesn't matter – I'm winning again," said Jake.

"I don't think so," Lizzie shook her head. "I've almost reached Neptune so I'm in the lead."

And sure enough, when Jake checked his scanner, Lizzie's ship was indeed ahead of him. Jake just couldn't understand it.

"Computer, go to the maximum possible speed," ordered Jake. "I'm not going to lose this race – I'm *not*!"

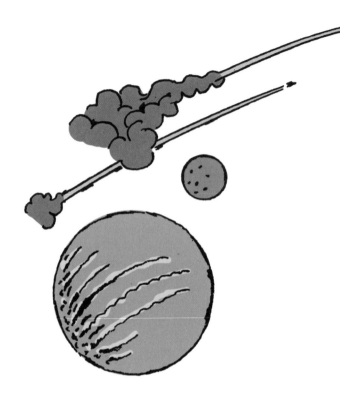

Jake's ship raced past Uranus, towards Neptune. He soon passed Lizzie's ship and headed on towards Pluto. Jake wasn't going to take any chances this time. He wasn't going to slow down until he got back to the space station. No way was

Lizzie going to pass him again.

Jake zipped round Pluto and started making his way back to the Astra space station. He had no idea how Lizzie managed to keep passing him. What was this secret weapon she had told him about? How could any secret

weapon be better than diamond
fuel? Jake scanned the area
again as he neared Neptune on
his return journey. His space
communicator beeped at him.
Moments later Lizzie's face
appeared.

"Come on, Jake. I thought
you'd be able to keep up with me

at least," Lizzie teased.

"What d'you mean?" said Jake.

"I'm coming up to the rings of Saturn," Lizzie told him. "You're going to have to do better than this!"

"How are you doing it?" Jake asked, bewildered. "How d'you keep managing to pass me? I don't even see you until you're ahead of me."

"That's thanks to my secret
weapon. Besides, space is a
big place. I don't have to take
exactly the same route as you,"
Lizzie told him.

"But . . ."

"See you back at the space station," Lizzie smiled.

"Computer, maximum speed back home," Jake commanded.

"We have been travelling at maximum speed for the last five minutes and forty-four seconds," the computer replied.

Jake sped past Saturn, raced past Jupiter, zoomed past Mars and screeched to a halt back in

docking-bay three on the space station. But it didn't make any difference. By the time he landed, Lizzie was already there, waiting for him. He had been beaten.

Chapter Five
The Secret Weapon

"I want to see this secret weapon," Jake demanded.

"D'you admit that I beat you?" Lizzie asked.

"Yes . . ." Jake said in a tiny voice.

"I can't hear you."

"YES!" Jake shouted. "Now can I see your secret weapon?"

"I don't think so," Lizzie said, considering carefully.

"Oh, but . . . but I'm bursting to know how you managed to beat me," Jake protested.

"If you tell everyone that I beat you, I'll think about it," Lizzie grinned.

Later on that day Lizzie and
her friends, Naren and Sarah and
Darla, all sat down for lunch.
Lizzie looked out of the view-
window and smiled at all the
stars around them. She loved
living on the Astra space station –

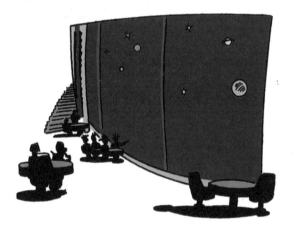

there was always something
new and exciting going on. And
today was a particularly good
day! Jake had been beaten!

"Has Jake guessed how we did it yet?" asked Naren.

Lizzie shook her head. "I feel a big guilty about the way we beat him. After all, we did cheat."

"No, we didn't. We just used our imaginations – that's all!" laughed Sarah.

"Besides, he was the one who tried to fix the race," Darla pointed out.

"Anyway, you were all brilliant!" said Lizzie. "I couldn't have done it without you."

Just then Jake appeared, with an expression on his face that none of them had ever seen before. For once, he wasn't smirking.

"Listen everyone!" Jake shouted out. The school dining-hall went very quiet. "This morning Lizzie and I had a race out to Pluto and back and Lizzie beat me. I lost!"

Everyone started clapping!
The whole school knew about
Jake's boasting, and this was the
first time he'd admitted he wasn't
perfect! Jake sat down at Lizzie's
table. "Now Lizzie, please, please
tell me how you did it."

Lizzie looked around the table at her friends. Should she or shouldn't she?

"Well, if you must know . . ." she began.

Jake leaned closer.

"I didn't race you – not really," Lizzie admitted.

"What d'you mean?" frowned Jake.

"I mean, I got as far as Mars and turned back," said Lizzie.

"But I saw your ship. First you were ahead of me at Jupiter and then I had to overtake you again

at Neptune," said Jake. "And on the way back, you were ahead of me again at Saturn."

"No, I wasn't." Lizzie smiled. "You passed *Sarah's* ship at Jupiter and you passed *Naren's* ship at

61

Neptune. And on the way back,
you passed *Darla's* ship at Saturn.
One good thing about all of us
having old ships is that they all
look the same. I just came back
here and pretended it was me all
the time."

"So . . . so it wasn't you . . ."
Jake was amazed.

"Nope! My friends were my secret weapon," said Lizzie

Jake leapt to his feet. "But that's not fair. I'm going to tell everyone . . ."

"How you fixed my engine so there was no way I could beat you?" Lizzie asked. "How you couldn't even race against me fair and square without cheating?"

Jake stared at her.

"How did you find out about that?"

"A little comet told me!" Lizzie replied. "And the next time you have a race, don't cheat! You might find you actually win!"

THE END

Colour First Readers

Welcome to Colour First Readers. The following pages are intended for any adults (parents, relatives, teachers) who may buy these books to share the stories with youngsters. The pages explain a little about the different stages of learning to read and offer some suggestions about how best to support children at a very important point in their reading development.

Children start to learn about reading as soon as someone reads a book aloud to them when they are babies. Book-loving babies grow into toddlers who enjoy sitting on a lap listening to a story, looking at pictures or joining in with familiar words. Young children who have listened to stories start school with an expectation of enjoyment from books and this positive outlook helps as they are taught to read in the more formal context of school.

Cracking the code

Before they can enjoy reading for and to themselves, all children have to learn how to crack the alphabetic code and make meaning out of the lines and squiggles we call letters and punctuation. Some lucky pupils find the process of learning to read undemanding; some find it very hard.

Most children, within two or three years, become confident at working out what is written on the page. During this time they will probably read collections of books which are graded; that is, the books introduce a few new words and increase in length, thus helping youngsters gradually to build up their growing ability to work out the words and understand basic meanings.

Eventually, children will reach a crucial point when, without any extra help, they can decode words in an entire book, albeit a short one. They then enter the next phase of becoming a reader.

Making meaning

It is essential, at this point, that children stop seeing progress as gradually 'climbing a ladder' of books of ever-increasing difficulty. There is a transition stage between building word recognition skills and enjoying reading a story. Up until now, success has depended on getting the words right but to get pleasure from reading to themselves, children need to fully comprehend the content of what they read. Comprehension will only be reached if focus is put on understanding meaning and that can only happen if the reader is not hesitant when decoding. At this fragile, transition stage, decoding should be so easy that it slowly becomes automatic. Reading a book with ease enables children to get lost in the story, to enjoy the unfolding narrative at the same time as perfecting their newly learned word recognition skills.

At this stage in their reading development, children need to:

- Practice their newly established early decoding skills at a level which eventually enables them to do it automatically

- Concentrate on making sensible meanings from the words they decode

- Develop their ability to understand when meanings are 'between the lines' and other use of literary language

- Be introduced, very gradually, to longer books in order to build up stamina as readers

In other words, new readers need books that are well within their reading ability and that offer easy encounters with humour, inference, plot-twists etc. In the past, there have been very few children's books that provided children with these vital experiences at an early stage. Indeed, some children had to leap from highly controlled teaching materials to junior novels.

This experience often led to reluctance in youngsters who were not yet confident enough to tackle longer books.

Matching the books to reading development

Colour First Readers fill the gap between early reading and children's literature and, in doing so, support inexperienced readers at a vital time in their reading development. Reading aloud to children continues to be very important even after children have learned to read and, as they are well written by popular children's authors, Colour First Readers are great to read aloud. The stories provide plenty of opportunities for adults to demonstrate different voices or expression and, in a short time, give lots to talk about and enjoy together.

Each book in the series combines a number of highly beneficial features, including:

- Well-written and enjoyable stories by popular children's authors

- Unthreatening amounts of print on a page

- Unrestricted but accessible vocabularies

- A wide interest age to suit the different ages at which children might reach the transition stage of reading development

- Different sorts of stories – traditional, set in the past, present or future, real life and fantasy, comic and serious, adventures, mysteries etc.

- A range of engaging illustrations by different illustrators

- Stories which are as good to read aloud to children as they are to be read alone

All in all, Colour First Readers are to be welcomed for children throughout the early primary school years – not only for learning to read but also as a series of good stories to be shared by everyone.
I like to think that the word 'Readers' in the title of this series refers to the many young children who will enjoy these books on their journey to becoming lifelong bookworms.

Prue Goodwin
Honorary Fellow of the University of Reading

Helping children to enjoy *Space Race*

If a child can read a page or two fluently, without struggling with the words at all, then he/she should be able to read this book alone. However, children are all different and need different levels of support to help them become confident enough to read a book to themselves.

Some young readers will not need any help to get going; they can just get on with enjoying the story. Others may lack confidence and need help getting into the story. For these children, it may help if you talk about what might happen in the book.

Explore the title, cover and first few illustrations with them, making comments about any clues to what might happen in the story.

Read the first chapter aloud together. Don't make it a chore. If they are still reluctant to read alone, share the whole book with them, making it an enjoyable experience.

Before reading

The story of Lizzie and her spaceship is set in the future on a Space Station called Astra. If children are unfamiliar with science fiction, it would be a good idea to explain that some writers make up what might happen in the future. Nobody really knows what might happen so an author can use their imagination to create new places, inventions and people.

During reading

Asking questions about a story can be really helpful to support understanding but don't ask too many – and don't make it into a test on what happens in the story. Relate the questions to the child's own experiences and imagination.

For example, ask: 'Do you know anyone who is always showing off and bragging like Jake?'; and 'Do you think Lizzie can really beat Jake in a race?'

Responding to the book

If your child has enjoyed the story, it increases the fun by doing something creative in response. If possible, provide art materials and dressing up clothes so that they can make things, play at being characters, act out a scene or respond in some other way to the story.

Activities for children

If you have enjoyed reading this story, you could:

- Look the map of Our Solar System at the beginning of the book. All the planets – except Earth – are named after Roman gods. To learn more you could look up the planets or the gods on the Internet.

- Share the story with a friend and, by being Lizzie and Jake, make up the scene in chapter one when Jake is bragging about his spaceship. You can check what is said by reading from page 10 to page 19.

- Find the words on pages 8, 9 and 10 to fill in the spaces in these sentences:

  1. Jake was boasting about his brand ___ , _____ duper, f__ – ace, de_____ spaceship.

  2. He said, 'My new ship's fast because it runs on _____ fuel.

  3. Lizzie thought that Jake was so pleased with himself that he would ___ like a _____ .

  4. When Lizzie had had enough she said: 'Jake, I ___ my ship could ____ yours ___ ___.'

74

- Draw a map of the race from the Space Station to Pluto and back again. Draw each of the spaceships in the right places: Sarah's ship at Jupiter; Naren's ship at Neptune; Darla's ship at Saturn; and Lizzie's ship at Mars.

- Explain why you think Lizzie cheated in the race by asking her friends to help her. Do you think it was fair? Would you have cheated? Did Jake deserve it? Was it to teach Jake a lesson about bragging?

- Design your own spaceship adding any extra special features to it that you want. You could do a painting of it zooming through space past the planets and stars.